No Way Yirrikipayi!

By children from Milikapiti School, Melville Island,
with Alison Lester

Indigenous Literacy Foundation

Yirrikipayi was hungry
so he went hunting.

Yirrikipayi – Crocodile

Finally, Yirrikipayi grabbed a huge Taringa under a log.

He thought he had his dinner.

But the Taringa coiled around him,

squeezed tight, and said,

'No way, Yirrikipayi!

You're not eating me today.

I'm hungry too

so I'm eating YOU!'

And the Taringa ate Yirrikipayi up.

Taringa - Snake

He nearly caught a Nyarringari just past the swamp

but the Nyarringari said,

'No way, Yirrikipayi!

You're not eating me today.

I'm too loud and honky,

I'll make you feel wonky.'

Nyarringari - Magpie Goose

He snapped at a Pika beside the bush
but the Pika said,
'No way, Yirrikipayi!
You're not eating me today.
I'm too strong and fast,
you'll always come last.'

Pika - Horse

He just missed a Jipwajirringa amongst the long grass

but the Jipwajirringa said,

'No way, Yirrikipayi!

You're not eating me today.

I'm lumpy and jumpy,

I'll make you feel grumpy.'

Jipwajirringa – Wallaby

Yirrikipayi was sick of chasing troublesome
creatures in the ocean so he headed inland.

He found a Jarrangani in the mud
but the Jarrangani said,
'No way, Yirrikipayi!
You're not eating me today.
I'm too tough and strong,
I'll make you feel wrong.'

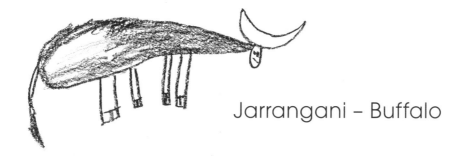

Jarrangani – Buffalo

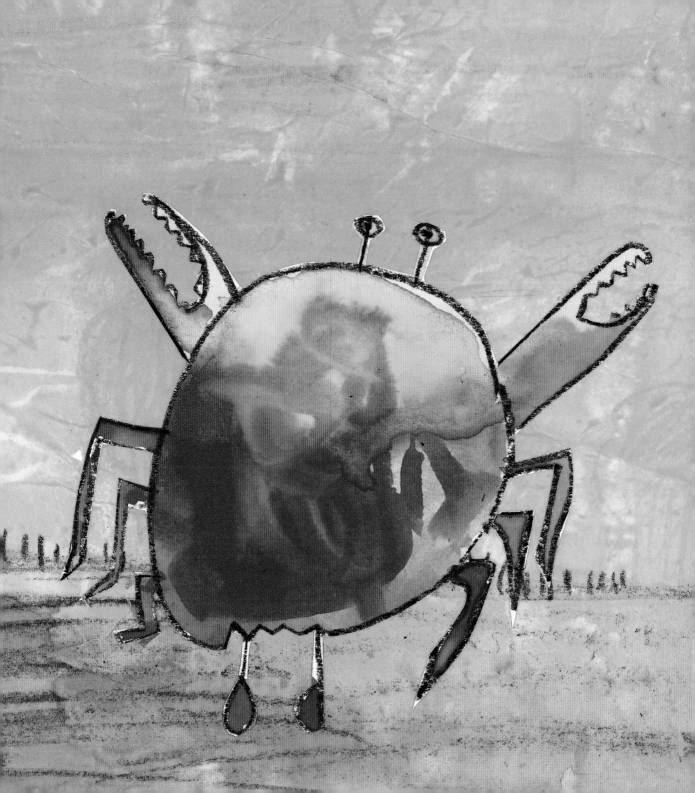

He chased a Kirimpika through the mangroves

but the Kirimpika said,

'No way, Yirrikipayi!

You're not eating me today.

I'm too quick and snappy,

I'll make you unhappy.'

Kirimpika - Crab

He lunged at an Arntirringa near the shore
but the Arntirringa said,
'No way, Yirrikipayi!
You're not eating me today.
I'm far too jelly
to be in your belly.'

Arntirringa - Jellyfish

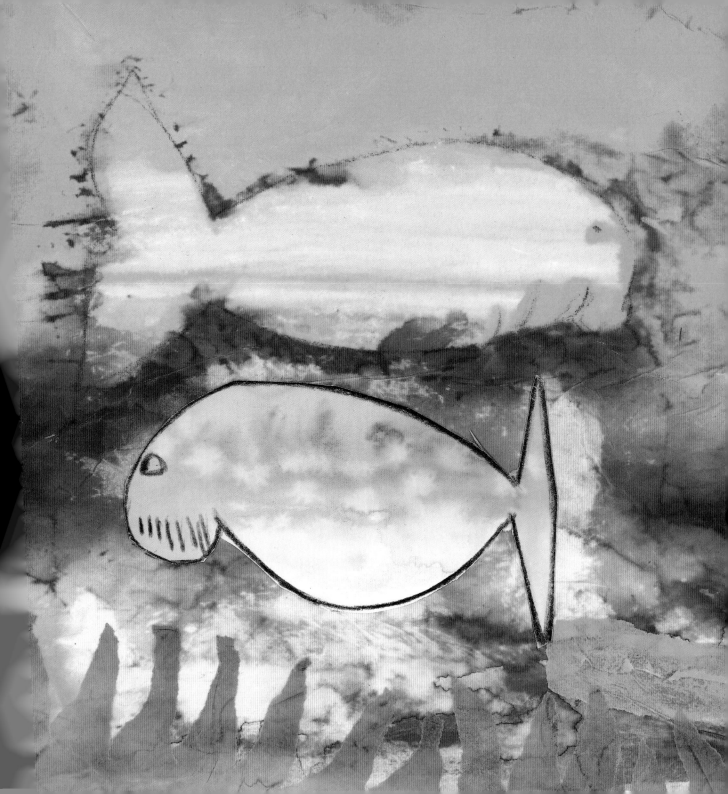

Yirrikipayi was getting hungrier and hungrier.

He chased a Marntuwunyini over the seagrass
but the Marntuwunyini said,
'No way, Yirrikipayi!
You're not eating me today.
My whiskery nose
will tickle your toes.'

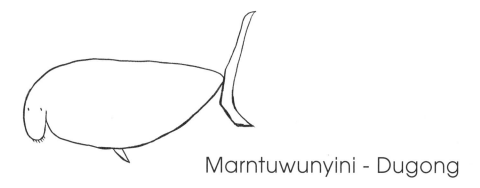

Marntuwunyini - Dugong

He went for a Kirluwarringa in the shallows

but the Kirluwarringa said,

'No way, Yirrikipayi!

You're not eating me today.

The spear in my tail

will cause you to wail.'

Kirluwarringa - Stingray

He surprised a Jarrakarlani on the reef

but the Jarrakarlani said,

'No way, Yirrikipayi!

You're not eating me today.

I've got a hard shell,

it'll make you unwell.'

Jarrakarlani - Turtle